We Don't Eat This!

by **Sue Graves** and **Alan Brown**

W

FRANKLIN WATTS
LONDON·SYDNEY

Jack and Ben went on holiday.
Mum and Dad went, too.

They stayed in a caravan
on Farmer Ted's farm.
They liked the farm and
they liked Farmer Ted.

One day, Farmer Ted was ill.

"I can't stay here," said Farmer Ted.

"I have to feed the animals."

"We can feed them for you,"
said Ben.

"Thank you," said Farmer Ted.

Jack and Ben went to feed
the hens.

"Hello, hens," said Jack.

"Here's some fish

for your breakfast."

The hens looked cross.

"We don't eat this!" they said.

Then Jack and Ben went to feed the horses.

"Hello, horses," said Ben.

He gave them a bone.

"We don't eat this!"
said the horses and
they looked cross.

Next Jack and Ben went to feed
the cats.

"Hello, cats," said Jack.

"Here is some corn
for your breakfast."

The cats looked cross.

"We don't eat this!" they said.

Jack and Ben went into
the field to feed the dogs.
"Hello, dogs," they said.
"Here is some hay
for your breakfast."

The dogs looked very cross.
"We don't eat this!"
they shouted.

All of the animals were cross.

"We don't eat this,"

they all shouted.

They went to see Farmer Ted.

Jack and Ben went to see
Farmer Ted, too.

"The animals are cross,"
said Farmer Ted. "You have to
give them food they like."

16

All the animals were happy.

"Thank you for your help,"

said Farmer Ted.

Story trail

Start

Start at the beginning of the story trail. Ask your child to retell the story in their own words, pointing to each picture in turn to recall the sequence of events.

Independent Reading

This series is designed to provide an opportunity for your child to read on their own. These notes are written for you to help your child choose a book and to read it independently.

In school, your child's teacher will often be using reading books which have been banded to support the process of learning to read. Use the book band colour your child is reading in school to help you make a good choice. *We Don't Eat This!* is a good choice for children reading at Green Band in their classroom to read independently.

The aim of independent reading is to read this book with ease, so that your child enjoys the story and relates it to their own experiences.

About the book

When Farmer Ted is ill, Jack and Ben try to help by feeding the animals, but they get it all mixed up!

Before reading

Help your child to learn how to make good choices by asking:
"Why did you choose this book? Why do you think you will enjoy it?"
Look at the cover together and ask: "What do you think the story will be about?" Support your child to think of what they already know about the story context. Read the title aloud and ask: "Who do you think might be saying 'We don't eat this!' on the cover?"
Remind your child that they can try to sound out the letters to make a word if they get stuck.
Decide together whether your child will read the story independently or read it aloud to you.

During reading

If reading aloud, support your child if they hesitate or ask for help by telling the word. Remind your child of what they know and what they can do independently.

If reading to themselves, remind your child that they can come and ask for your help if stuck.

After reading

Support comprehension by asking your child to tell you about the story. Use the story trail to encourage your child to retell the story in the right sequence, in their own words.

Help your child think about the messages in the book that go beyond the story and ask: "Do you think Ben and Jack were very helpful? Why/why not?"

Give your child a chance to respond to the story: "Did you have a favourite part? Have you ever got things mixed up when you were trying to help?"

Extending learning

Help your child understand the story structure by using the same story context and adding different elements. "Let's make up a new story about Jack and Ben helping out on the farm.

What job are they trying to help with? What might get mixed up?" In the classroom, your child's teacher may be teaching polysyllabic words (words with more than one syllable). There are many in this book that you could look at with your child, for example: hol/i/day, ca/ra/van, farm/er, an/i/mals, break/fast, shout/ed, happ/y.

Franklin Watts
First published in Great Britain in 2020
by The Watts Publishing Group

Series Editors: Jackie Hamley and Melanie Palmer
Series Advisors: Dr Sue Bodman and Glen Franklin
Series Designer: Peter Scoulding

A CIP catalogue record for this book is
available from the British Library.

ISBN 978 1 4451 7074 9 (hbk)
ISBN 978 1 4451 7073 2 (pbk)
ISBN 978 1 4451 7075 6 (library ebook)

Printed in China

Franklin Watts
An imprint of
Hachette Children's Group
Part of The Watts Publishing Group
Carmelite House
50 Victoria Embankment
London EC4Y 0DZ

An Hachette UK Company
www.hachette.co.uk

www.franklinwatts.co.uk